ANANSE'S FEAST
AN ASHANTI TALE

Retold by **Tololwa M. Mollel**
Illustrated by **Andrew Glass**

CLARION BOOKS/*New York*

**I wish to thank Mohammed Issaka from Ghana for his kind assistance
with some cultural points in the story.
—T.M.M.**

Clarion Books
a Houghton Mifflin Company imprint
215 Park Avenue South, New York, NY 10003
Text copyright © 1997 by Tolowa M. Mollel
Illustrations copyright © 1997 by Andrew Glass

The illustrations were executed in oil and colored pencil on paper.
The text was set in 16-point Meridian Medium.

www.houghtonmifflinbooks.com

Printed in Hong Kong

Library of Congress Cataloging-in-Publication Data

Mollel, Tololwa M. (Tololwa Marti)
Ananse's feast : an Ashanti tale / retold by Tololwa M. Mollel ;
illustrated by Andrew Glass.
p.   cm.
Summary: Unwilling to share his feast, Ananse the spider tricks Akye the turtle
so that he can eat all the food himself, but Akye find a way to get even.
ISBN 0-395-67402-6   PA ISBN 0-618-19598-X
1. Anansi (Legendary character)—Legends. [1. Anansi (Legendary character)—
Legends. 2. Ashanti (African people)—Folklore. 3. Folklore—Ghana.]
I. Glass, Andrew, ill. II. Title.
PZ8.1.M73An   1996
398.2'0967'0452544—dc20
[E]   95-17358
CIP
AC

SCP 10 9 8

To Stephen Arnold, and family —*T.M.M.*

For my pals Betsy and Larry —*A.G.*

The earth was hot and barren and no one had much to eat, except Ananse the Spider. Before the drought clever Ananse had stored away food from his farm, and now he decided to treat himself to a feast.

Ananse shut his door and windows and sealed all the cracks in the walls of his old hut.

"I don't want the delicious smell of my cooking to bring hungry visitors," he muttered.

But somehow the aroma of food escaped and reached Akye the Turtle, who was searching for something to eat on a dusty riverbed nearby.

"I'll drop in on my old friend Ananse," thought hungry Akye. "I'm sure he'll spare me a bite."

Ananse was setting the table when he heard a
knock on the door. He stood still and listened.
"Whoever it is will soon go away," he thought
hopefully.

The knocking didn't stop, however, and Ananse

had to open the door. He didn't want to share his feast with anyone. Yet when he saw his friend Akye, he couldn't bring himself to send him away.

"Oh, it is you, Akye," said Ananse, smiling. "Come in and be my guest!"

Akye stared at the mountain of food. He didn't
know where to start. "I'll eat the golden, crisp fried
plantain first," he thought. "How delicious it looks!
Oh, look at the steaming hot soft yam and the pepper
soup! No, I'll start on the fluffy coconut rice and the
creamy beans with ground peanuts."

He was reaching for the rice when Ananse stopped him. "Your hands are dirty!" he told Akye. "In my house, it is only good manners to wash your hands before eating."

Akye looked at his hands, dusty and dirty from his manner of walking on all fours. "Can I have some water to wash them?" he asked.

"I'm sorry, I've used up all the water," replied Ananse. "You must go and wash your hands at the river."

The river was dry except for a few puddles. Akye washed his hands thoroughly in one of them. And back he crawled,

a-kye-kye-die
a-kye-kye-die,

his empty stomach moaning, *Oyei-yaai oyei-yaai!* as he thought of the fluffy coconut rice and the creamy beans with ground peanuts.

But greedy Ananse had eaten up the rice and the beans.

"No matter," thought Akye. "I'll have the steaming hot soft yam and the pepper—"

"Look, your hands, you didn't wash them," Ananse said with a frown.

Akye looked at his dusty hands and shook his head. "Strange—I did wash them. Well, I'll go and wash them again."

At the river Akye rubbed, scrubbed, rinsed, and wiped his hands. Then up the riverbank he clambered,

a-kye-kye-die
a-kye-kye-die,

his empty stomach groaning, *Oyei-yai-yaai oyei-yai-yaai!* as he thought of the steaming hot soft yam and the pepper soup.

He got back to find selfish Ananse finishing up the yam and the soup.

"Your hands are still dirty!" mumbled Ananse.

"But I just washed them!" protested Akye.

"You don't seem to have done a good job of it," replied Ananse, laughing. "Go back to the river!"

By the time Akye returned from the river, cunning
Ananse had eaten all the food and was wearing a
big satisfied grin.

Akye suddenly realized how Ananse had tricked him. He only smiled, however, and said to well-fed Ananse, "Thank you for inviting me to the feast. I hope one day I can repay you."

A few days later, the drought ended. Rain came down. The earth bloomed and food crops burst forth. Rivers flowed, teeming with fish and crabs.

It rained so much that farms became swampy. The harvest was late, and Ananse, who was not a good fisherman, had little to eat. So he was delighted to receive an invitation to a feast at the turtle's home under the river.

21

Hungry Ananse arrived at the river dressed for the feast in a brilliant ceremonial robe. He climbed up a tall tree on the riverbank.

Then, straight as an arrow, he dived into the water. *Bul bul bul bul bul*, he sank.

23

He was too light to stay underwater, though.

And *bul bul bul bul bul*, he rose, floating back to the surface.

He climbed higher on the tree and dived again.

Bul bul bul bul bul, he sank.

Bul bul bul bul bul, he rose.

Then Ananse had an idea. "I know how I can get to the feast!" he exclaimed. He filled the enormous pockets of his robe with pebbles from the beach. Then he climbed to the very top of the tree and came streaking down.

Bul bul bul bul bul, he sank.

Bul bul bul bul bul, he sank.

Down to the feast!

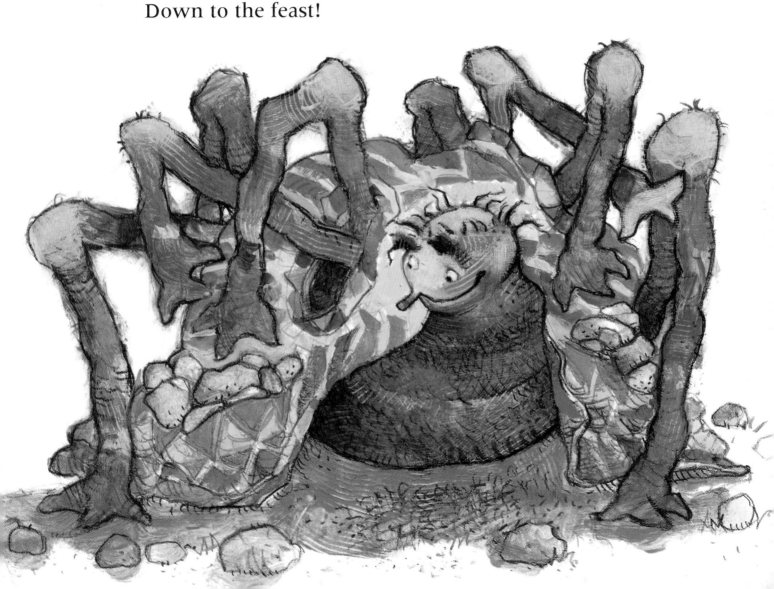

Akye was seated at a table laden with plump mounds of juicy, tender crabmeat, dressed in a brilliant ceremonial robe of his own. With his heavy shell, he had no trouble staying down.

The turtle noticed the bulging weight of pebbles in Ananse's pockets and touched the spider's robe admiringly.

"What a beautiful robe!" he said, and smiled. "But I suggest you take it off before we eat."

"What!" cried Ananse.

"In my house," Akye said sweetly, "it is only good manners to take off your robe before eating." And he began to slip out of his own robe.

Ananse couldn't let Akye think he was an ill-mannered guest. Reluctantly, he took off his robe. And although he tried hard to cling to the table . . .

Bul bul bul bul bul, he rose.
Bul bul bul bul bul, he rose.
Back to the surface!

Unable to return to the feast without his heavy robe, Ananse sat shivering on the bank, his empty stomach wailing,

Oyei-yai-yai-yaai!
Oyei-yai-yai-yaai!

as he thought of the plump mounds of juicy, tender crabmeat.

Some time later, well-fed Akye walked out of the river,

a-kye-kye-die
a-kye-kye-die.

With a big satisfied grin, he came to squat alongside his old friend Ananse.

"What a delicious feast that was," said Akye, rubbing his full belly with pleasure. "Thank you so much for coming. The meal would not have been the same without you. Let's make sure we have another feast soon!"

AUTHOR'S NOTE

A trickster is just what a storymaker needs: a character who makes things happen. Ananse the Spider does that aplenty. He is so famous, he has his own body of traditional tales. These tales are called Anansesem, "Spider Stories," among the Ashanti, Fante, and other ethnic groups who together make up the Akan peoples in the West African country of Ghana. Among many contradictory qualities, Ananse is a gluttonous schemer who enjoys making fools of others. At times, however, he suffers the taste of his own medicine.

a-kye-kye-die (AH cheh cheh dee eh): An Ashanti word for "turtle," which seemed to me to express the image of a turtle in motion. The turtle character's name, Akye (AH cheh), is a play on the same word.

Oyei-yaai! (OH yey yeah eye): Maasai-language expression meaning "O my mother!", an exclamation or lamentation uttered by someone in distress. I have taken artistic license in adapting that East African expression for this West African story.